Your Press-Out Models

S0-BNK-865

Inside this book are eighteen flying paper models. Press them out and make them up, following the instructions provided.

Sticking and folding

There are two different types of paper folds: hill folds and valley folds. These are indicated by guide lines printed on the models. There are also guide lines to mark where to use glue.

··················	Stick here using all-purpose glue
- - - - - - - -	Hill folds form a peak
-·-·-·-·-·	Valley folds are V-shaped

Setting the wing angle

The models have 5 types of wing angles. The wing angles stabilise the gliders when flying. It is important to follow the glue points with the wing supports and keep the same angles on each side of the wing.

Make sure the wing angles are the same.

Launching the gliders

Hold the glider's body, throw firmly, and let go.
If launched correctly, it will fly straight ahead.
If launched incorrectly, the glider will either stall or dive.

A stall may occur if it is launched too quickly.

A dive may occur if it is launched too slowly.

Flying the gliders

You can correct the flight by adding weight (sticky tack) to the head or the tail/feet.

Add weight to the head to correct a stall.

Add weight to the tail to correct a dive.

Models by David Hawcock and Simon Ward • Text by Katherine Sully
Design by Jessica Moon • Illustrations by Nigel Dobbyn and Arpad Olbey
Packaged for Arcturus by Infinite Jest Ltd.
www.hawcockbooks.com

All other images from Shutterstock

SPIRIT DRAGON

Dragon Data
Latin name: *Draco animalis*
Size: 4–10 m (13–32 ft) long
Wingspan: 12 m (40 ft)
Top speed: 170 km/h (105 mph)
Life span: 100 years
Population estimate: 1,000

The most elusive creature in the Draco family is *Draco animalis*, the Asian spirit dragon. You can only see the spirit dragon out of the corner of your eye. If you look at it directly, the dragon seems to disappear.

Blue moon
The spirit dragon only becomes completely visible during a lunar eclipse. There is great excitement amongst dragon spotters when this occurs, but it only happens about twice a year.

Long tail feathers help the spirit dragon turn swiftly in midflight, causing unexpected breezes in the bamboo forests.

The age of a spirit dragon can be estimated from the length of its whiskers. This dragon is about 40 years old.

Scales on the dragon's body reflect light. When shed naturally, dragon scales gleam and glitter in the light, and are often made into necklaces and rings.

Many memories
Legend has it that the spirit dragon carries the memories of all its ancestors and can remember the first humans on the planet.

Optical illusion
Scientists have worked out why the spirit dragon is just so hard to see. They believe that the dragon's scales act like mirrors, camouflaging it against the clouds and sky.

Spirit dragon song

The spirit dragon sings as it flies. Its song carries vast distances across the sky, attracting other spirit dragons. When two spirit dragons meet, they circle each other in the sky singing different verses.

Share the feast

Spirit-dragon songs have many meanings. Sometimes they issue warnings to rivals to stay away. Other songs are invitations to join a feast. Mostly they are about how much wiser dragons are than people.

The spirit dragon only feeds at night. It is particular fond of the very rare moonlight moths, which taste like honey.

The dragon's long jaw whiskers can detect movements in air currents, which is how it finds its prey.

Fast food

With their long, flexible bodies, spirit dragons are able to twist and turn in the air, snapping up moths, bats, fireflies, and sometimes even an unwary owl!

Spirit Dragon

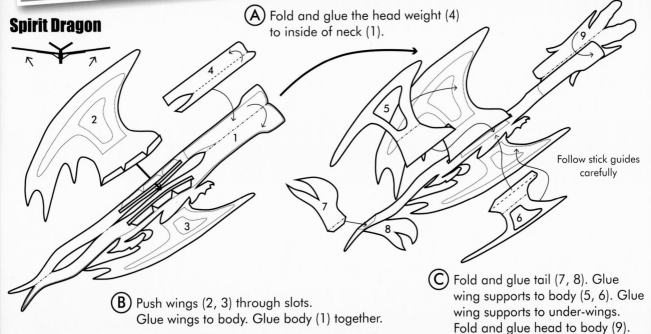

A Fold and glue the head weight (4) to inside of neck (1).

Follow stick guides carefully

B Push wings (2, 3) through slots. Glue wings to body. Glue body (1) together.

C Fold and glue tail (7, 8). Glue wing supports to body (5, 6). Glue wing supports to under-wings. Fold and glue head to body (9).

FOREST DRAGON

The savage forest dragon, *Draco silvarum*, is the only known tree-dwelling dragon. It lives high in the forest canopy, building its nest across the tops of several trees.

The forest dragon is a good flier, taking to the skies to survey its territory. In the forest, it keeps its wings tightly folded to avoid damaging them.

Tree crawlers

Despite its large size, the forest dragon is a stealthy hunter. It hides in the treetops until a deer walks underneath and then it drops like a stone to snatch its prey.

A forest dragon's teeth are strong enough to crunch through a deer's skull. The deer's antlers make great toothpicks.

Pretty nest

The forest dragon is particularly fond of white-tailed deer. It keeps the tails to line its nest.

The green scales of the forest dragon act as camouflage, helping it to hide among trees.

Warning sound

When fearing for the safety of their young, forest dragons produce a warning howl before attacking. If you are in a forest and hear a noise like an angry wild boar, then you should run fast—you might have disturbed a forest dragon... or a wild boar.

Dragon Data

Latin name: Draco silvarum
Size: 3 m (10 ft) long
Wingspan: 8 m (26 ft)
Top speed: 70 km/h (45 mph)
Life span: 200 years
Population estimate: 2,500

Forest life

You won't often see a forest dragon's nest, as they are built high in the tree canopy. Dragons decorate their nests with the things they find in the forest such as bones, poisonous berries, and moss.

Finding food

The forest dragon eats much the same food as bears, including deer, squirrels, and rabbits. Often a dragon will snatch food away from a bear—and then eat the bear too!

Powerful muscles in its front and back legs allow this dragon to climb trees with ease.

Dragons are often blamed for causing forest fires. Being fireproof, the dragons are unharmed by the flames.

Winter sleep

During the winter, forest dragons gather together to hibernate in caves. They return in spring to rebuild their nests. If they spot a nest they like better, they fight other dragons for it!

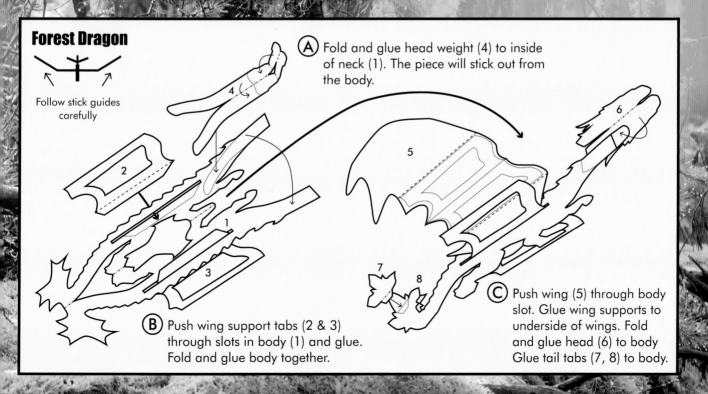

Forest Dragon

Follow stick guides carefully

(A) Fold and glue head weight (4) to inside of neck (1). The piece will stick out from the body.

(B) Push wing support tabs (2 & 3) through slots in body (1) and glue. Fold and glue body together.

(C) Push wing (5) through body slot. Glue wing supports to underside of wings. Fold and glue head (6) to body. Glue tail tabs (7, 8) to body.

GEM DRAGON

A deep cave dweller, the gem dragon, *Draco gemmae*, is solitary, and seldom seen. This is probably a good thing, as it is known to be bad-temepered and rather stupid.

Dragon Data
Latin name: *Draco gemmae*
Size: 4.5 m (15 ft) long
Wingspan: 11 m (36 ft)
Top speed: 120 km/h (75 mph)
Life span: 40 years
Population estimate: 5,000

Rainbow skin
When the gem dragon feels calm, it appears mostly green and blue. If it is threatened or angry, it turns red and pink.

Wing claws help the gem dragon to scramble over slippery rocks deep within underground caverns.

When underground, the dragon keeps its wings tucked tightly into its sides. Every night, it emerges outside to stretch its wings.

Light force
The gem dragon can produce a beam of light from its eyes so it can see where its going. But if it is angry, it can increase the power of its eyes until the beam can cut through rock.

The dragon's skin is tough to protect it from sharp rocks.

Mines
Miners digging for minerals live in fear of breaking through to a gem dragon's lair. They often stop and listen for any sign that a gem dragon is about.

Life underground

The gem dragon feeds on minerals in deep seams of rock. It stays underground during the day but comes to the surface at night. Daylight is too dazzling for the gem dragon.

Finding food

Graphite and quartz form most of the gem dragon's diet. Using its eye beams, the gem dragon blasts minerals from the rock before chewing them. The dragon occasionally eats shellfish found in underground lakes, mistaking them for shiny pebbles.

Crystals like these look deliciou
a gem dragon. When visiting ca
it is recommended you cover u
sparkly rings or necklaces.

The simple gem dragon sometimes attacks its own tail, confusing it with the head of another dragon in the dark.

Rock crushers

The teeth of the gem dragon are made of diamond, the hardest substance on Earth. If you see large bitemarks in a boulder, it is a sign you are near a gem dragon cave.

Gem Dragon

Follow stick guides carefully

Ⓐ Push wing support tabs (2, 3) through slots in body (1) and glue. Concertina fold and glue head weights to inside of head. Glue body together.

Ⓑ Glue tail tabs (5, 6) to body (1). Push wing (4) through slot in body. Glue wing supports to wing.

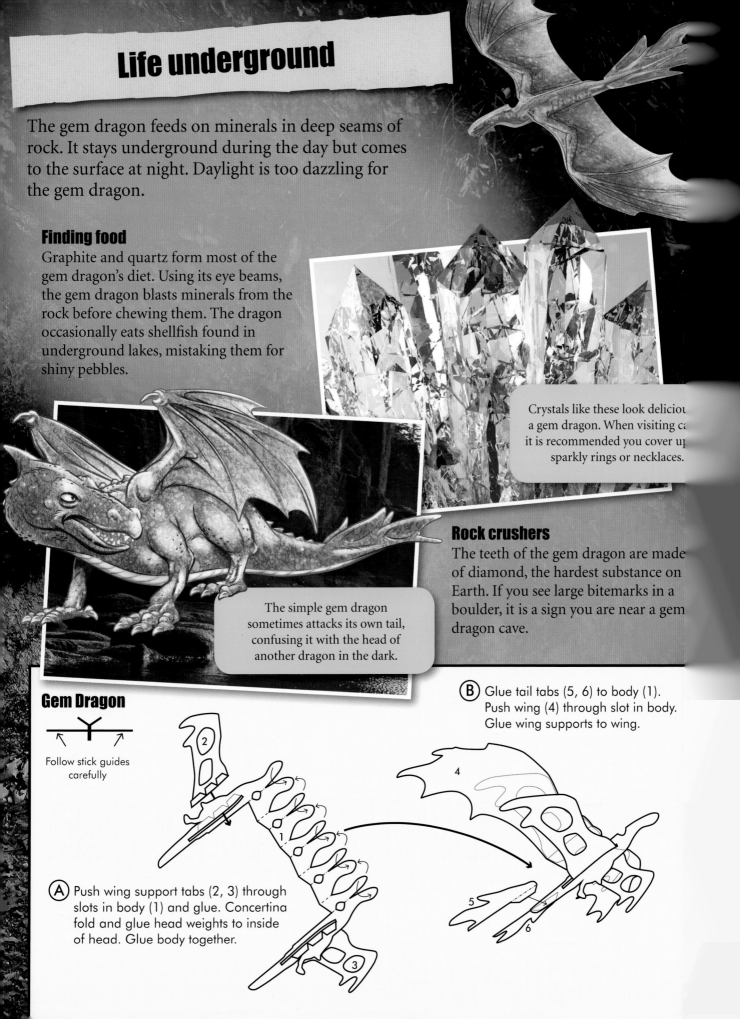

MOUNTAIN DRAGON

The powerful, quick-tempered mountain dragon, *Draco montis*, has a distinctive red hide that matches its fiery breath. It lives in the icy caves of remote peaks, where mountaineers fear to tread.

The mountain dragon's pointed teeth can pierce the toughest skin. Its beak is strong enough to crush bones.

Cave dwelling

Every day, the dragon has to revamp its cave. First, it clears the snow with a blast of flame, then it breathes on the cave walls until they glow red-hot. The cave is then snug and warm until the rocks lose their heat.

This dragon swoops down and snatches up its prey in its sharp claws. It rarely misses.

Warrior dragon

With four head horns and jaw spikes protecting its head, the mountain dragon is a fearsome sight to its prey and even other species of dragon.

One heavy blow from the mountain dragon's whale-like tail can cause a dangerous avalanche from the high mountain peaks.

Dragon Data

Latin name: *Draco montis*
Size: 5 m (16.5 ft) long
Wingspan: 13 m (43 ft)
Top speed: 107 km/h (66 mph)
Life span: 500 years
Population estimate: 200

Night hunter

As darkness falls, the mountain dragon emerges from its cave to hunt black bears, snow leopards, and mountain goats.

Strike after dark

This nocturnal hunter tracks by moonlight, following paw prints in snow and sensing the heat given off by its prey. The safest place to hide is in the forests further down the slopes.

High-rise nest

The mountain dragon lays a single, leathery egg during the spring, which takes 18 months to hatch. It chooses the most remote, inaccessible place to build its nest.

A mountain dragon's eyes glow an eerie red at night as they detect the warmth of their prey far below.

The mountain dragon defends its nest ferociously against hungry yeti, who try to steal the egg.

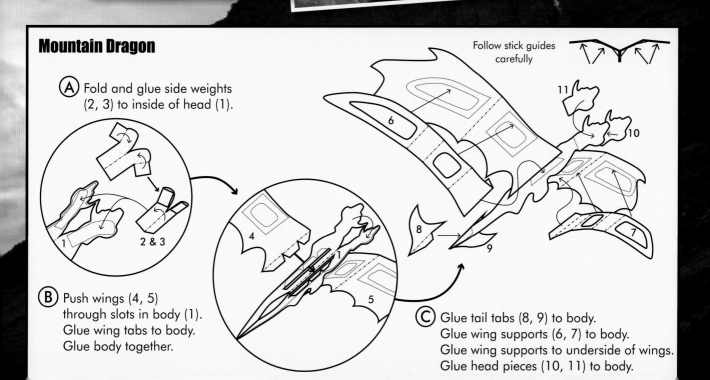

Mountain Dragon

Follow stick guides carefully

(A) Fold and glue side weights (2, 3) to inside of head (1).

(B) Push wings (4, 5) through slots in body (1). Glue wing tabs to body. Glue body together.

(C) Glue tail tabs (8, 9) to body. Glue wing supports (6, 7) to body. Glue wing supports to underside of wings. Glue head pieces (10, 11) to body.

SEA SERPENT

Dragon Data

Latin name: Draco serpens maris
Size: 13.5 m (44 ft) long
Wingspan: 30 m (98.5 ft)
Top speed: 48 km/h (30 mph)
Life span: 500 years
Population estimate: 250

For generations, sailors told tales of monstrous eels. At the time they were dismissed as wild exaggeration, but scientists now know the sailors had seen *Draco serpens maris*, a powerful sea serpent.

Water weaver

The sea serpent has a long, spiny, elastic backbone which allows it to weave through the air and water like a giant snake.

The sea serpent eats giant squid, octopus, and whales. It senses them with its forked tongue.

Once wrapped in the serpent's flexible and muscular tail there is no escape for sea creatures or small boats!

Wide kite-like wings allow the sea serpent to glide for long distances.

Grabbing a meal

In the past, fishermen often hunted the same prey as sea serpents. The serpent would smash their boats with its tail to prevent them from stealing its meal.

By air or sea

The sea serpent can hunt from the air or in the water. By air, it skims the water surface and scoops up prey in its huge talons. Underwater, it patrols the depths, coiling its prey in its tail.

The next generation

During the first 50 years of its life, the sea serpent lives deep underwater. It is only when it reaches its adult size that it emerges from the sea to hunt in air as well as water.

Nesting ground

Like a turtle, the female sea serpent chooses a sandy beach to lay her eggs. The bright yellow eggs can be spotted easily, so the dragon stays close to guard them until they hatch.

Sea serpent eggs hatch as the high tide washes over them during a full moon.

The sea serpent fears only one creature in the water—the mighty kraken, terror of ancient mariners.

Kraken

The sea serpent is prey for the kraken. This giant, squid-like creature can snatch a serpent from its low flight using its tentacles. Suckers along the kraken's arms hold its victim fast as it digests its huge meal.

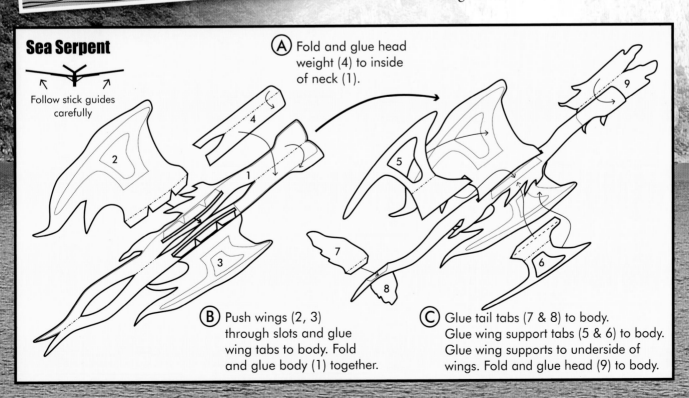

Sea Serpent

Follow stick guides carefully

(A) Fold and glue head weight (4) to inside of neck (1).

(B) Push wings (2, 3) through slots and glue wing tabs to body. Fold and glue body (1) together.

(C) Glue tail tabs (7 & 8) to body. Glue wing support tabs (5 & 6) to body. Glue wing supports to underside of wings. Fold and glue head (9) to body.

LUCKY DRAGON

The lucky dragon, *Draco felix*, is the smallest member of the Draco family. Covered in glowing, golden scales, this shy rainforest creature is said to bring you good fortune if you spot it.

The lucky dragon has short arms and legs and long claws that it uses to scramble up and down tree trunks.

Golden myth
Legend has it that if you manage to catch one of these elusive dragons, it will turn to solid gold in your hands. More likely is that it will give you a nasty bite!

On display
Because of the moist air in the rainforest, the lucky dragon has to open out its wings to dry before flying.

The lucky dragon has red and gold eyes that can hypnotise its prey.

When feeling threatened, the dragon raises its tail to make itself look bigger.

Rainforest home
Rainforests are an ideal habitat for the lucky dragon. The heat and humidity suit their lazy, treetop lifestyle. They spend much of their time roosting in the canopy, snacking on passing frogs and insects.

Dragon Data
Latin name: Draco felix
Size: 1 m (3 ft) long
Wingspan: 1.5 m (5 ft)
Top speed: 45 km/h (28 mph)
Life span: 90 years
Population estimate: 4,000

Rules of attraction

The lucky dragon's eyes swirl with red and yellow. Once its prey looks into its eyes, they seem to go into a trance. The dragon inches forward until it is close enough to pounce!

The dragon's hypnotic eyes keep it safe from predators, as well as making prey much easier to catch.

Look into my eyes

Even people have been caught in the hypnotic eyes of the lucky dragon. Those who have got close to a dragon report a complete blank in their memory, lasting several hours.

Lucky egg

After an egg is laid, the mother and father stay close to the nest to guard it. Young dragons often play together, chasing each other through the treetops and swinging upside-down on branches.

The eggs of lucky dragons have a solid gold shell. Treasure hunters travel deep into the jungle in search of them... but few return.

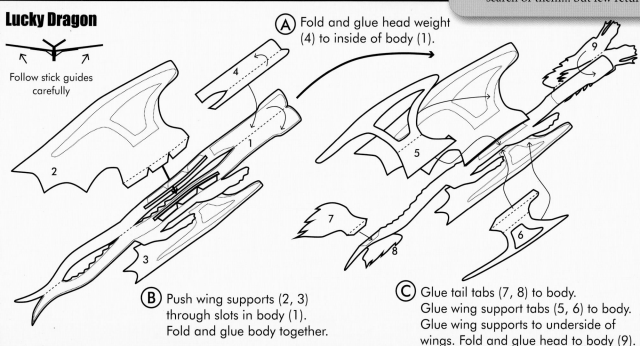

Lucky Dragon

Follow stick guides carefully

Ⓐ Fold and glue head weight (4) to inside of body (1).

Ⓑ Push wing supports (2, 3) through slots in body (1).
Fold and glue body together.

Ⓒ Glue tail tabs (7, 8) to body.
Glue wing support tabs (5, 6) to body.
Glue wing supports to underside of wings. Fold and glue head to body (9).

WYVERN DRAGON

Dragon Data

Latin name: Draco vulgaris
Size: 1.5 m (5 ft) long
Wingspan: 3 m (10 ft)
Top speed: 75 km/h (47 mph)
Life span: 100 years
Population estimate: 2,000

One of only a few friendly dragons, the wyvern, *Draco vulgaris*, is a small, two-legged dragon. Its love of shiny things sometimes brings it into conflict with humans.

Playful dragon

Wyverns are sociable dragons, and live in small groups. They enjoy playing tag and rough-and-tumble games in the air with other wyverns.

The wyvern has two horns that point backward. They look impressive but they are not very useful for fighting.

The wyvern's wings are slightly transparent. They clap them together to call to each other.

Mostly harmless

Despite its fierce appearance and reputation, the wyvern is a placid, playful creature. Humans are much more of a danger to wyverns than they are to us.

Chimney stacks

Wyvern nests are commonly found on the chimneys of abandoned houses and castles. The wyverns start a fire below to keep their eggs warm.

Treasure seeker

The wyvern is probably the least threatening of all the Draco family, and yet it has also been the most hunted. This is because wyverns are known to collect gold, precious gems, and other treasure.

Thieves have been known to capture young wyverns and train them to creep down chimneys and steal treasure.

Treasure-hunter

Wyverns love gold, silver, and precious jewels, but only because they are shiny. They also love mirrors, and some even become entranced by the reflection of sunlight on a still lake.

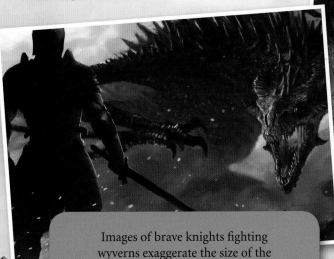

Images of brave knights fighting wyverns exaggerate the size of the dragons. Most are not much bigger than a dog!

Shiny

In olden times, knights were employed to guard treasure as it was moved from place to place. Unfortunately, the knights' shiny chainmail was more likely to attract wyverns than scare them away!

Wyvern Dragon

Follow stick guides carefully

(A) Push wing support tabs (2, 3) through slots in body (1) and glue. Concertina fold and glue head weights to inside of head. Glue body together.

(B) Glue tail tabs (5, 6) to body. Push wing (4) through slot. Glue wing supports to wing. Glue head (7, 8) to body.

1
2
3
4
5
6
7
8

ICE DRAGON

Draco glaciai is the only ice-breathing dragon. It lives in cold northern lands. With the widest wingspan of all the Draco family, the ice dragon's beating wings create a freezing wind.

Dragon Data

Latin name: Draco glaciai
Size: 30 m (100 ft) long
Wingspan: 65 m (213 ft)
Top speed: 63 km/h (40 mph)
Life span: 1,000 years
Population estimate: no more than 90

The ice dragon's blood contains a natural antifreeze.

Double horns, shaped like icicles, make the ice dragon easy to identify.

Ice caves

During the winter, the ice dragon spends its time hunting. In the summer months, it seeks out an ice cave to hibernate. During this deep sleep, the ice dragon's heartbeat slows to one beat per day.

This spiky tail makes a powerful weapon for knocking out orcas or walruses.

Freezing plunge

The ice dragon can swim in the freezing-cold ocean water and hold its breath for up to 10 minutes. One hunting technique is to lurk beneath the surface of the ice, then burst up to devour unwary seals.

Dragon of legend

Carvings of ice dragons have been discovered on the remains of ancient Viking warships. Old sagas describe ice dragons dive-bombing fishing boats to raid them for their cargo of freshly caught fish.

Icy breath

As it flies over the ocean, the ice dragon is always on the lookout for prey. When it spots a large fish, the dragon freezes the water with its icy breath, trapping the prey in ice.

One lick from the ice dragon's long tongue will drain a living creature of all warmth.

It is said that Vikings were forced to explore and settle in other lands to escape the deadly attacks of ice dragons.

Icy nest

The ice dragon lays its eggs in a snowy nest and then leaves them. The snow keeps the eggs warm until the dracolings are ready to hatch.

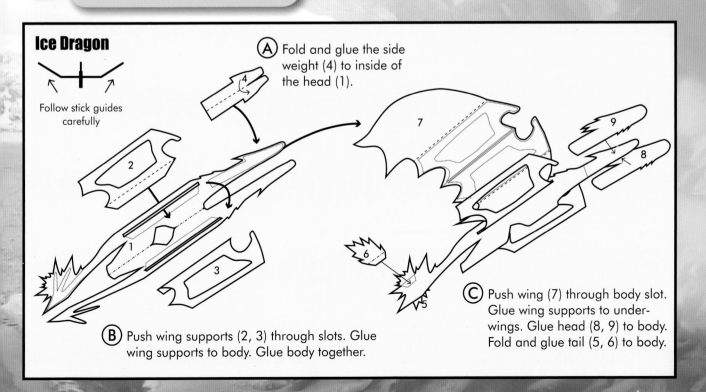

Ice Dragon

Follow stick guides carefully

A Fold and glue the side weight (4) to inside of the head (1).

B Push wing supports (2, 3) through slots. Glue wing supports to body. Glue body together.

C Push wing (7) through body slot. Glue wing supports to under-wings. Glue head (8, 9) to body. Fold and glue tail (5, 6) to body.

FIRE DRAGON

The distinctive *Draco ignis* is one of the most feared of the fire-breathing dragons. Powerful and easily angered, it will attack any creature that gets too close.

Fiery den

This dragon makes its home in volcanoes or cracks in the Earth's crust where molten lava is near the surface.

A fire dragon can breathe a jet of flame as long as its body. It has caused many devastating fires.

If you get past the the dragon's fire, you'll next need to survive its claws. They are as long as a banana and as sharp as a sword.

Restless beast

The fire dragon spends most of its time circling above its volcano, only coming in to land during rainstorms. When it rains the dragon will bury itself deep in the heart of its volcano and sleep until the shower is over.

Flight and fight

The weather dragon is the natural enemy of the fire dragon. If these two dragons come to blows, they create a spectacular lightning storm.

Dragon Data

Latin name: Draco ignis
Size: 16.5 m (55 ft) long
Wingspan: 37 m (120 ft)
Top speed: 87 km/h (54 mph)
Life span: 500 years
Population estimate: 1,500

Flame grilled

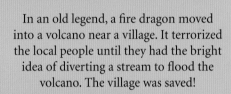

As it patrols the air above its volcano, the fire dragon searches for its next meal. It eats birds—the bigger the better. It is a formidable aerial hunter.

Barbecue diner

The fire dragon catches its prey in mid-air. Flying up behind, it breathes a fireball which kills and cooks its prey in one go.

Large birds such as vultures, eagles, and condors make good meals for the fire dragon. It avoids eating bats, which upset its stomach and make it belch flames.

In an old legend, a fire dragon moved into a volcano near a village. It terrorized the local people until they had the bright idea of diverting a stream to flood the volcano. The village was saved!

Home sweet volcano

Young fire dragons must find their own volcano to live in, and many travel vast distances to find an empty one—or they fight an older dragon for their volcano!

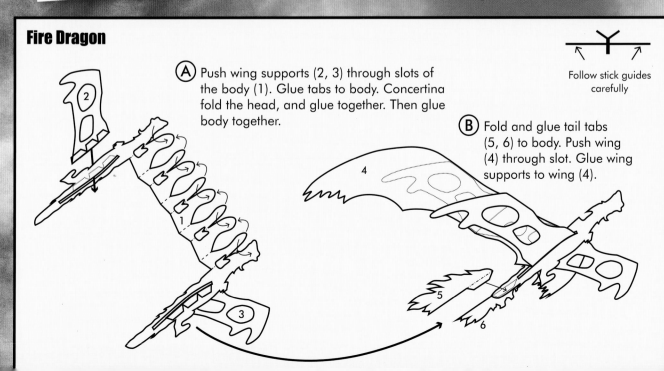

Fire Dragon

(A) Push wing supports (2, 3) through slots of the body (1). Glue tabs to body. Concertina fold the head, and glue together. Then glue body together.

(B) Fold and glue tail tabs (5, 6) to body. Push wing (4) through slot. Glue wing supports to wing (4).

Follow stick guides carefully

METALLIC DRAGON

Dragon Data
Latin name: Draco metallicus
Size: 15 m (50 ft) long
Wingspan: 36 m (118 ft)
Top speed: 98 km/h (61 mph)
Life span: 120 years
Population estimate: 50

The most powerful of all the dragons, the metallic dragon, *Draco metallicus*, lives in ore-rich mountain ranges. These days, it is also found near villages and towns, scavenging for metal.

Heavy metal
With a body covered in metal plates, this dragon is a like a flying tank. Its metal hide reflects sunlight, bright enough to dazzle potential enemies.

Instead of blood, the metallic dragon has molten steel running through its veins.

Its long tongue is magnetic. If it licks the ground, anything metal will stick to it.

Its powerful wings creak when they beat up and down, like a machine that needs oiling.

Fire breath
Metal dragons breath fire. They focus their flame on a rock until the iron-ore turns to liquid and runs out of the stone. The dragon then licks up the molten metal with its very long tongue.

Cast-iron stomachs
The metallic dragon has several stomachs, each with its own digesting properties, so anything it eats can be processed quickly.

Metallic menace

For centuries there has been conflict between people and the metallic dragon. Miners digging for metals disturb the homes of the dragon, and in retaliation it smashes their machines.

Dragon doses

From sunrise to sunset, the metallic dragon must sleep to digest its food. It chooses a cool, shady spot so the sun doesn't overheat its metal body.

When this dragon dies, its body decays but its metal scales remain.

Safe and dry

The greatest fear of the metallic dragon is rust. It hates getting wet, and is never far from a cave or other shelter. A rusty dragon finds it hard to fly, or even walk.

In medieval times, metallic dragons were hunted for their hides. Their tough skins were used to make weapons and shields.

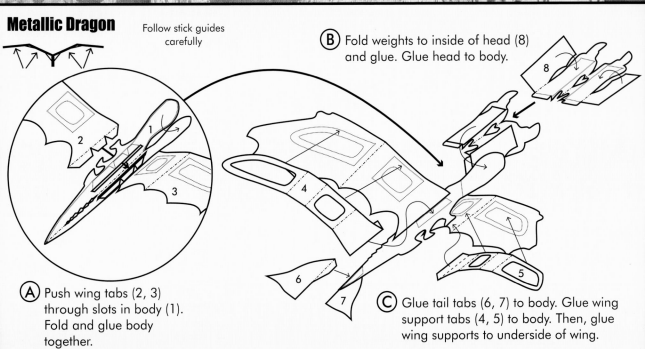

Metallic Dragon

Follow stick guides carefully

(A) Push wing tabs (2, 3) through slots in body (1). Fold and glue body together.

(B) Fold weights to inside of head (8) and glue. Glue head to body.

(C) Glue tail tabs (6, 7) to body. Glue wing support tabs (4, 5) to body. Then, glue wing supports to underside of wing.

WEATHER DRAGON

Dragon Data

Latin name: Draco tempestatis
Size: 16.5 m (54 ft) long
Wingspan: 38 m (125 ft)
Top speed: 117 km/h (73 mph)
Life span: 120 years
Population estimate: 2,000

Many extreme storms are the work of the weather dragon, *Draco tempestatis*. One of the swiftest members of the Draco family, the weather dragon spends almost its whole life in the air.

By flying in a circle with its wings at full spread, the weather dragon generates a massive hurricane.

Voice of doom

The dragon's low growl sounds like the rumble of thunder. It can be heard up to ten miles away.

By staying in the air, the dragon is unaffected by lightning bolts, which pass through its body to hit the ground far below.

Thunderbolts

The weather dragon has a special chamber behind its nose where it can build up an electrical charge. This is then released from its mouth as a deadly lightening bolt.

The dragon communicates to others of its kind by using its tail to sculpt clouds into mysterious shapes.

Weather disturbance

Spending most of its time at the edge of space, the weather dragon dips into the atmosphere to feed. This is the time when weather systems become most disturbed.

Life above the clouds

Scientists believe that the dragon spends much of its time above the clouds, following the prevailing winds.

Gassy diet

The weather dragon exists largely on a diet of oxygen, hydrogen, and helium. These, combined with other gases in the atmosphere, provide all of its nutrients.

The weather dragon's natural enemy is the fire dragon. Their battles are the cause of violent storms.

When weather dragons gather together, the resulting storms can destroy crops and houses for miles around.

Creating clouds

Male weather dragons show off to females by creating lightning storms. Only males strong enough to make hurricanes will keep the female dragon's interest.

Weather Dragon   Follow stick guides carefully

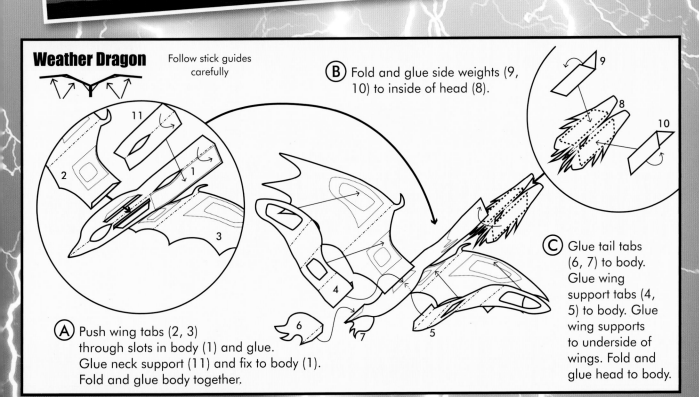

(B) Fold and glue side weights (9, 10) to inside of head (8).

(A) Push wing tabs (2, 3) through slots in body (1) and glue. Glue neck support (11) and fix to body (1). Fold and glue body together.

(C) Glue tail tabs (6, 7) to body. Glue wing support tabs (4, 5) to body. Glue wing supports to underside of wings. Fold and glue head to body.

BABY DRAGONS

Baby dragons are playful, curious, and quick to learn. When they hatch, dracolings look like miniature versions of adults. They leave the nest almost immediately to look for food, but come back to it to sleep, for safety.

Dragon Data

Latin name: not applicable
Egg size: 1-4 m (3-13 ft) long
Wingspan: 2-6 m (6.5-20 ft)
Fly: 1-5 years
Reach maturity: 5-100 years
Clutch size: 1-5 eggs

Dragon's egg

A dragon's egg has a tough, leathery shell that protects the growing baby.

Dragons usually lay between one and five eggs in each clutch.

Eggs can be buried in sand or laid in a nest of rocks or tree branches.

Hatching

Inside the egg, the baby dragon, called a dracoling, feeds on the iron-rich yolk. It grows inside the egg until it is ready to hatch. Once hatched, it rests with its wings outstretched to dry.

Dracolings

The dracoling loses its nose horn once it has hatched. Its head and jaw horns do not appear until it becomes an adult. The age of a dracoling can be estimated from the length of its head horns.

The dracoling has a special nose horn it uses to break through the tough shell of the egg.

Flying solo

Once the dracoling has dried its wings and rested after the struggle of hatching, it is ready to fly. This is a natural instinct and doesn't need to be taught.

Shedding skin

Within hours of hatching, the dracoling will shed its skin like a snake. Snakes sometimes move into discarded dragon skin for protection.

Play-fighting

Dracolings love to play-fight. It prepares them for hunting in adulthood. They practice pouncing, snatching from the air, and rolling, often trying out their skills on unsuspecting wildlife.

Dracolings need a lot of sleep, so mind your step on the beach or forest floor!

A dracoling hatching from a clutch of eggs loves to tussle with its brothers and sisters.

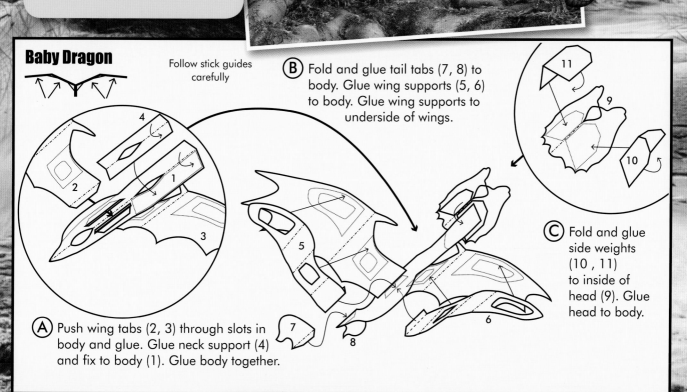

Baby Dragon

Follow stick guides carefully

A Push wing tabs (2, 3) through slots in body and glue. Glue neck support (4) and fix to body (1). Glue body together.

B Fold and glue tail tabs (7, 8) to body. Glue wing supports (5, 6) to body. Glue wing supports to underside of wings.

C Fold and glue side weights (10, 11) to inside of head (9). Glue head to body.

GRIFFIN

The griffin has the head of an eagle and the body of a lion. To fly, the griffin must first break into a run. It then launches itself into the air with a powerful beat of its magnificent wings.

The feathers are surprisingly soft. Pillows made from griffin feathers are said to bring good dreams.

Powerful hybrid

The griffin is a top-level predator. It can snatch prey from the air using its front talons, then tear flesh with its beak and the claws on its back feet.

A griffin's tail contains threads of gold but no one has dared get close enough to steal them.

Flight fright

The griffin flies at a great height, using its incredibly sharp vision to scan the horizon for wild horses and deer. Once it has located its victim, it folds back its wings and dives, snatching up its prey before it even sees the griffin's shadow.

Guardians of treasure

Most griffin pairs live in the mountains. They react fiercely if their nests or young are threatened, but are otherwise fairly peaceful.

Mythical Beast Data

Size: 2 m (6 ft) long (not including tail)
Wingspan: 7 m (23 ft)
Top speed: 50 km/h (31 mph)
Life span: 30 years
Population estimate: 2,000

Majestic beast

The griffin is known for its power and strength. Compared to dragons, it is relatively small, but it is more than a match for them because of its speed and bravery.

Enemies

The griffin has many enemies. Young animals are sometimes attacked by bears, wolves, or mountain lions, but they also face danger from ogres, basilisks, and giant serpents.

Loyal pairs

Griffin pairs are very loyal and stay together for life. The male griffin makes a nest out of twigs and feathers, and decorates it with precious gems. Griffins rarely leave their nest unattended as they are highly prized by thieving ogres.

Griffin statues denote strength and leadership. Statues are rarely accurate, however, as few people have seen a living griffin.

The griffin is known for its great courage and will fight a basilisk or serpent to the death.

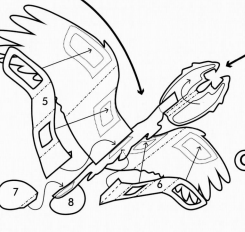

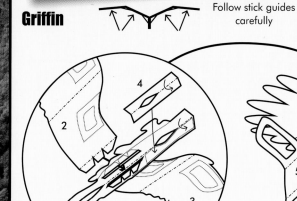

Griffin

Follow stick guides carefully

A Push wing tabs (2, 3) through slots in body (1) and glue. Fold and glue neck support (4) to body, then fold and glue body together.

B Fold and glue weights (10, 11) to inside of head (9).

C Glue tail tabs (7, 8) to tail. Glue wing supports (5, 6) to body. Glue wing supports to underside of wings. Fold and glue head to body.

THUNDERBIRD

The mighty Thunderbird is found in North America. It features in many stories passed down through generations of Native Americans. It is considered a sacred spirit and a force of nature.

Mythical Beast Data

Size: 5.5 m (18 ft) long
Wingspan: 15 m (50 ft)
Top speed: 160 km/h (100 mph)
Life span: immortal
Population estimate: one

The Thunderbird lives on a great mountain. In one legend, it flooded the Earth so that only the mountaintops remained above water.

Mighty bird

The Thunderbird is said to carry the rainbow across the sky. But it has an angry side too, sometimes bringing bad weather and turning people to stone.

Powerful claws can easily lift a fully grown buffalo.

A curved pointed beak and flashing eyes give the Thunderbird a fierce expression.

Kindly creature

A powerful symbol and an intelligent being, the Thunderbird shows kindness to people in legend. It fought the serpents of the underworld and supplied whale meat to the starving people of the north.

Life-giver

In different traditions, the Thunderbird has varying powers. In some accounts, the arrival of the Thunderbird marks the awakening of spring. In others, the Thunderbird carries a lake on its back from which rain falls.

Shapeshifter

The Thunderbird sometimes disguises itself as a masked, cloaked human with great healing powers. In this form it can summon rain and call on other spirits.

Thunder and lightning

By clapping its mighty wings, the Thunderbird creates thunder. This is how it got its name. It can also produce lightning bolts from its eyes.

The legendary bird features in many totems in Thunderbird Park, British Columbia.

Totems

Totems were symbols of the upper spirit world. In some totems, the Thunderbird is shown as a birdman.

As master of the storm, the great Thunderbird is to be feared and respected.

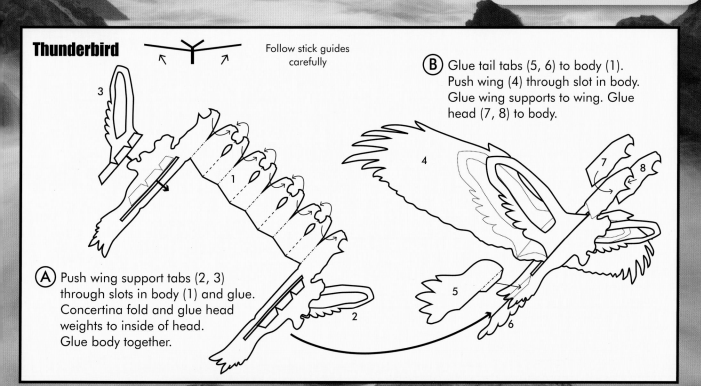

Thunderbird

Follow stick guides carefully

(A) Push wing support tabs (2, 3) through slots in body (1) and glue. Concertina fold and glue head weights to inside of head. Glue body together.

(B) Glue tail tabs (5, 6) to body (1). Push wing (4) through slot in body. Glue wing supports to wing. Glue head (7, 8) to body.

SPHINX

The sphinx is a ruthless protector of lost cities and ancient tombs. It can turn its body to stone and appear lifeless, but if it detects a threat it will spring to life and challenge the intruder.

Mythical Beast Data

Size: 40 m (130 ft) long
Wingspan: 90 m (295 ft)
Top speed: 50 km/h (30 mph)
Life span: unknown, but probably immortal
Population estimate: 5–10

Broad wings allow the sphinx to circle slowly above its desert home.

The sphinx prefers to face east, to enjoy the sunrise.

The sphinx is fond of pearls, and often keeps one between its paws.

Mix and match
The sphinx has the head of a human pharaoh, the body and tail of a golden lion, and the wings of an eagle.

Lost in sand
As the sphinx can spend centuries utterly still, they are often covered in sand. Nobody knows how many are hiding in the Earth's deserts.

Guardian of the gates
If you wish to pass through gates guarded by a sphinx first you must answer its riddle. If you get the answer wrong it will carry you to a volcano and drop you in.

Riddle of the sphinx

Anyone wishing to pass the sphinx of Thebes had to answer this riddle: "What walks on four feet in the morning, two feet in the afternoon, and three feet in the evening?"

Deadly riddle

The Greek king Oedipus answered the sphinx of Thebes' riddle correctly: a person. We crawl on all fours as a baby at the beginning of our lives, walk on two feet as adults in the middle of our lives, and walk with a cane in old age.

Death of a sphinx

Legend tells that the sphinx of Thebes was so angry when Oedipus answered the riddle that she turned herself to stone permanently.

There are both male and female sphinxes, but little is known about baby sphinxlings.

The sphinx of Giza is the guardian of the pyramids. It appears to be made of stone, but could it just be waiting?

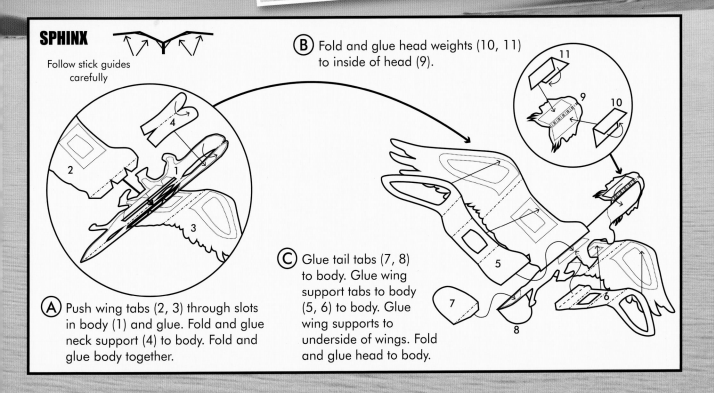

SPHINX

Follow stick guides carefully

(A) Push wing tabs (2, 3) through slots in body (1) and glue. Fold and glue neck support (4) to body. Fold and glue body together.

(B) Fold and glue head weights (10, 11) to inside of head (9).

(C) Glue tail tabs (7, 8) to body. Glue wing support tabs to body (5, 6) to body. Glue wing supports to underside of wings. Fold and glue head to body.

Phoenix

Mythical Beast Data

Size: 2.8 m (6.5 ft) long

Wingspan: 3 m (10 ft)

Top speed: 107 km/h (67 mph)

Life span: 500–1,000 years
before rebirth

Population estimate:
unknown

Born and reborn from the fire, the phoenix is part-bird, part-spirit. It is one of the few truly immortal creatures, able to regenerate itself at the end of its long lifespan.

Long feathers form a crest on the phoenix's head.

The phoenix's feathers are red-hot. If you find one, you can use it as a source of heat—once you find a way to carry it home.

The phoenix has magnificent plumage of yellow, orange, and red. Sparks of pure gold can also be seen in the feathers.

Healing tears

The tears of a phoenix can magically heal all wounds. Alchemists also believe that phoenix tears, added to the right potion, will give you everlasting life. Nobody has discovered the correct recipe yet, but alchemists continue to work on it.

Sweet song

Although it is very rare to see a phoenix, you may hear its melodious five-note song. It is said that the sun god Apollo halted his chariot to listen to a phoenix.

Fragrant nest

The phoenix makes its nest in the heart of a smouldering fire. It lays a single golden egg.

Rising from the ashes

The phoenix lives for centuries before bursting into flames until it is completely destroyed. It rises from the ashes as a young bird again.

Royal boast

In the past, some royals claimed they had a captured phoenix living in their palace. It might have been true... but who would dare to contradict a king?

Because of its power to be born again from its own destruction, the phoenix is a symbol of transformation and rebirth.

The phoenix has the ability to turn its body into flames, and then become a bird again.

No peeking!

A glowing halo around the phoenix makes it difficult to see clearly. If it flies at night, it is sometimes mistaken for a shooting star.

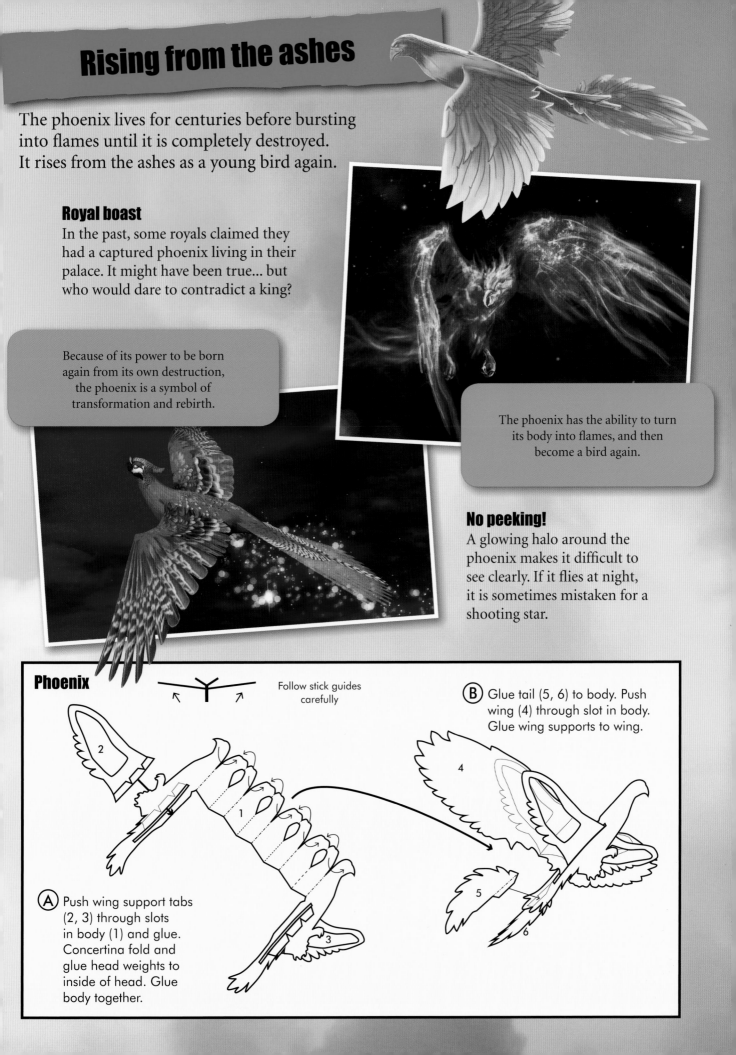

Phoenix

Follow stick guides carefully

Ⓐ Push wing support tabs (2, 3) through slots in body (1) and glue. Concertina fold and glue head weights to inside of head. Glue body together.

Ⓑ Glue tail (5, 6) to body. Push wing (4) through slot in body. Glue wing supports to wing.

PEGASUS

Pegasus is a beautiful horse with white wings and a white coat. The ancient Greeks had many stories about his adventures, as as he was ridden by two legendary heroes, Perseus and Bellerophon.

Mythical Beast Data

Size: 3 m (10 ft) long
Wingspan: 8 m (26 ft)
Top speed: 45 km/h (28 mph)
Life span: immortal
Population estimate: one

Practically perfect

This strong, winged horse is the perfect steed. He is kind, faithful, and brave.

Looking for a horn? You must mistaking Pegasus for the legendary unicorn!

His wings are covered with soft white feathers and are similar in shape to an eagle.

Early life

Pegasus was born of two gods. The sea god Poseidon and snake-haired Medusa were Pegasus' parents. Pegasus was adopted by the Muses, goddesses of the arts.

Pegasus gallops, then leaps into the air to take off.

Fountain of words

When the hero Perseus killed the monstrous Medusa, Pegasus sprang from her body.

Legend tells us that wherever Pegasus' hoof strikes the ground, water springs up. He was responsible for creating a fountain on Mount Helicon. The spring water is said to turn anyone who drinks it into a poet.

Winged adventure

While drinking the spring waters at Hippocrene, Pegasus was captured by the warrior, Bellerophon. Bellerophon tamed Pegasus using a golden bridle that had special powers.

Fighting the Chimera

Bellerophon rode Pegasus to fight the Chimera, a ferocious double-headed monster. Bellerophon slew the Chimera, but his boasting angered Zeus, king of the gods. Zeus sent a gadfly to sting Pegasus, and Bellerophon fell from the horse to his death.

The constellation, Pegasus, is one of the brightest in the night sky.

The fire-breathing Chimera is just one of the horrible beasts that Pegasus had to face with his human riders.

A true star

Pegasus became a messenger to Zeus, delivering thunderbolts to Mount Olympus, the home of the gods. As a reward, Zeus made Pegasus immortal, as a constellation in the night sky.

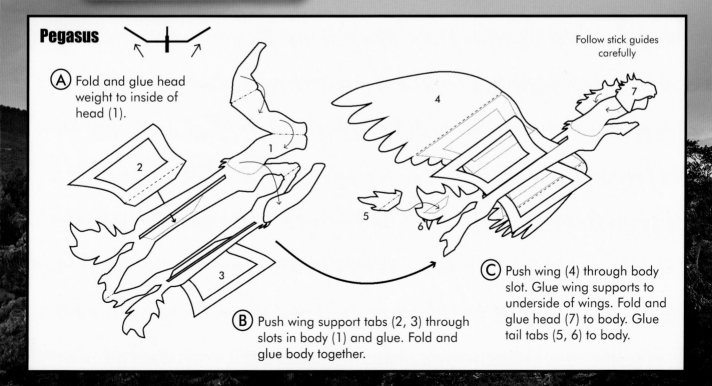

Pegasus

Follow stick guides carefully

(A) Fold and glue head weight to inside of head (1).

4

1

2

7

5

6

3

(B) Push wing support tabs (2, 3) through slots in body (1) and glue. Fold and glue body together.

(C) Push wing (4) through body slot. Glue wing supports to underside of wings. Fold and glue head (7) to body. Glue tail tabs (5, 6) to body.

ROC

This giant bird has a wingspan so wide that it is said to block out the sun when it flies. A great wind is created when it flaps its wings, strong enough to drive clouds before it.

Mythical Beast Data

Size: 15 m (48 ft) long
Wingspan: 30 m (100 ft)
Top speed: 141 km/h (88 mph)
Life span: 50 years
Population estimate: 20

Powerful hunter

The Roc has enormous strength. It carries its prey into the sky, dropping it to the ground before swooping down to feed on the carcass.

Even the Roc's feathers are huge. Each wingfeather is the size of a small child.

The Roc's talons are strong enough to carry a small elephant or a large deer.

Roc

Follow stick guides carefully

(A) Push wing support tabs (2, 3) through slots in body (1) and glue. Concertina fold and glue head weights to inside of head (1). Glue body together.

(B) Glue tail (5, 6) to body (1). Push wing (4) through slot in body. Glue wing supports to wing. Fold and glue head (7) to body.